If
you take
a careful look,
you'll see
how
creatures
in this book
are
CAMOUFLAGED
and out
of view—
although
they're
right
in
front
of
you.

To April
Ruth Heller
1987

how to hide a butterfly

& OTHER INSECTS

BY RUTH HELLER

D1504929

Grosset & Dunlap

Copyright © 1985 by Ruth Heller. All rig   ), a member of The Putnam
Publishing Group, New York. Printed in Italy. Published simultaneously in Canada. Library of Congress
Catalog Card Number 85-70287   ISBN 0-448-10478-4   A B C D E F G H I J

The
BUTTERFLY
that you
see
here

just
folds
its wings...

to
disappear.

This
MOTH will do
a different
thing.

It
covers up each underwing,
so all that anyone can see...

is
the
bark
upon
a
tree.

The
INCHWORM's
feet are at
both ends.

To move, it stretches

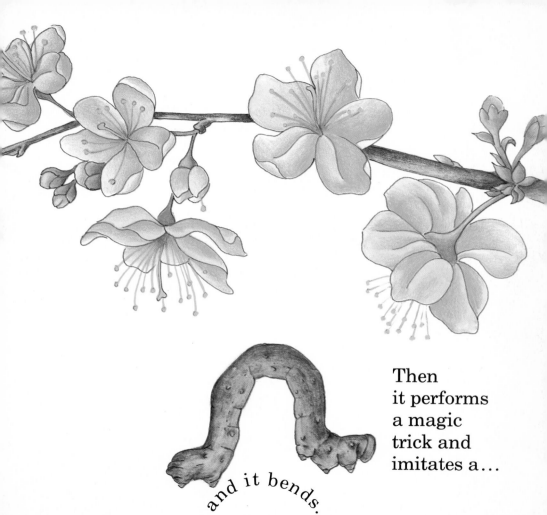

Then
it performs
a magic
trick and
imitates a...

and it bends.

twig
or
stick.

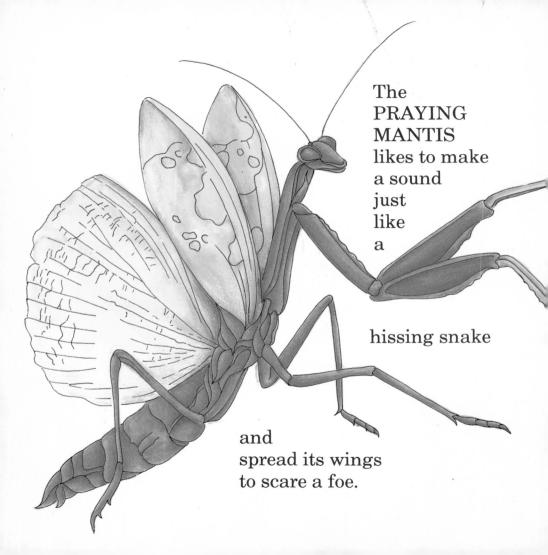

The
PRAYING
MANTIS
likes to make
a sound
just
like
a

hissing snake

and
spread its wings
to scare a foe.

It
somehow
always
seems
to know
it won't
be
seen
when
dining
where the
leaves...

are
green.

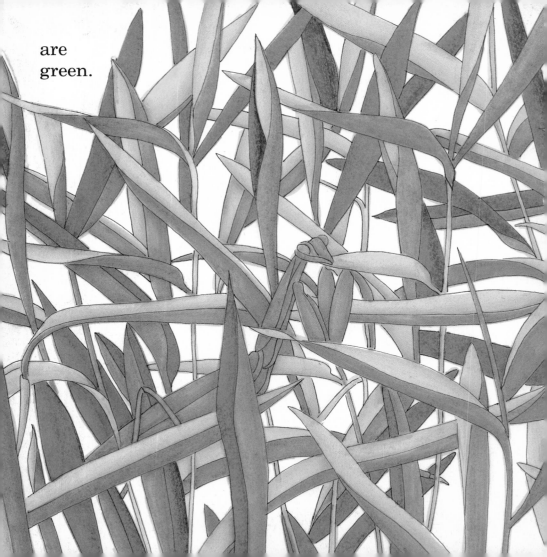

GRASSHOPPERS
leap

sometimes
three feet,

and
what
you
thought
that
you just saw
now looks
more
like...

a
bit
of
straw.

This
FLY
you
see
looks
like
a
bee

and
thereby
fools
its
enemy,
but
here's
a clue
I'll tell
to you:
FLIES only have
one pair of wings,
while bees…

you see,

have
two.

SPIDERS
are not
insects,
as
I'm
sure
you
know,
but
this
SPIDER
is a hider,

and she's very, very slow
to change herself
to yellow
and then to pink
or white,
depending on the flower
that she decides is right,
where she can wait
to catch her prey
and still be…

out
of
sight.